GREMLINS

GIZMO'S 12 DAYS OF CHRISTMAS

WRITTEN BY ANDREA ROBINSON

ILLUSTRATED BY JJ HARRISON

SAN RAFAEL • LOS ANGELES • LONDON

A note to readers:

This book is read to the tune of "The Twelve Days of Christmas." Each line that **LOOKS LIKE THIS** is the start of a new verse.

Each line that ***LOOKS LIKE THIS*** should be emphasized like the line in the song, "five golden rings."

ON THE FIRST DAY OF CHRISTMAS, MY FATHER GAVE TO ME,
A Mogwai bought from Mr. Wing.

ON THE SECOND DAY OF CHRISTMAS, THE MORNING IT DID SEE,

One broken car

And a neighbor's Gremlin theory.

ON THE SECOND DAY OF CHRISTMAS, LATE IN THE AFTERNOON,
Ran into Deagle,
But at least Kate is looking at me.

ON THE THIRD DAY OF CHRISTMAS, MY FATHER SAID TO ME:

No bright lights,
Don't get him wet,
And please always feed him early!

AM
12 00

ON THE FOURTH DAY OF CHRISTMAS, WHILE GIZMO WATCHED TV,
One clumsy kid,
One spilled jar
(Oops, that's a rule),
And Gizmo's screaming like a banshee.

ON THE FIFTH DAY OF CHRISTMAS, MY MOGWAI GAVE TO ME,

FIVE MORE MOGWAI!

One with a stripe,
Four cohorts,
All kinds of mean . . .

And **HEY!** Who did this to **BARNEY?**
COME ON, LET'S GET YOU DOWN.

ON THE SIXTH DAY OF CHRISTMAS, THE MORNING BROUGHT TO ME,
Six creepy pod things . . .
ALL HATCHING NOW!

One teacher dead,
This seems bad.
Oops, Mom's at home,
Better go and see what's happening.

FLEA
TICK

ON THE SEVENTH DAY OF CHRISTMAS,
In the kitchen I did see:
Gremlin feet a-spinning,
Green goo a-dripping—
THAT MICROWAVE'S RUINED!

Mom's on the floor—
What to do?
Cool! Mounted swords
And a dead Gremlin in the fir tree!

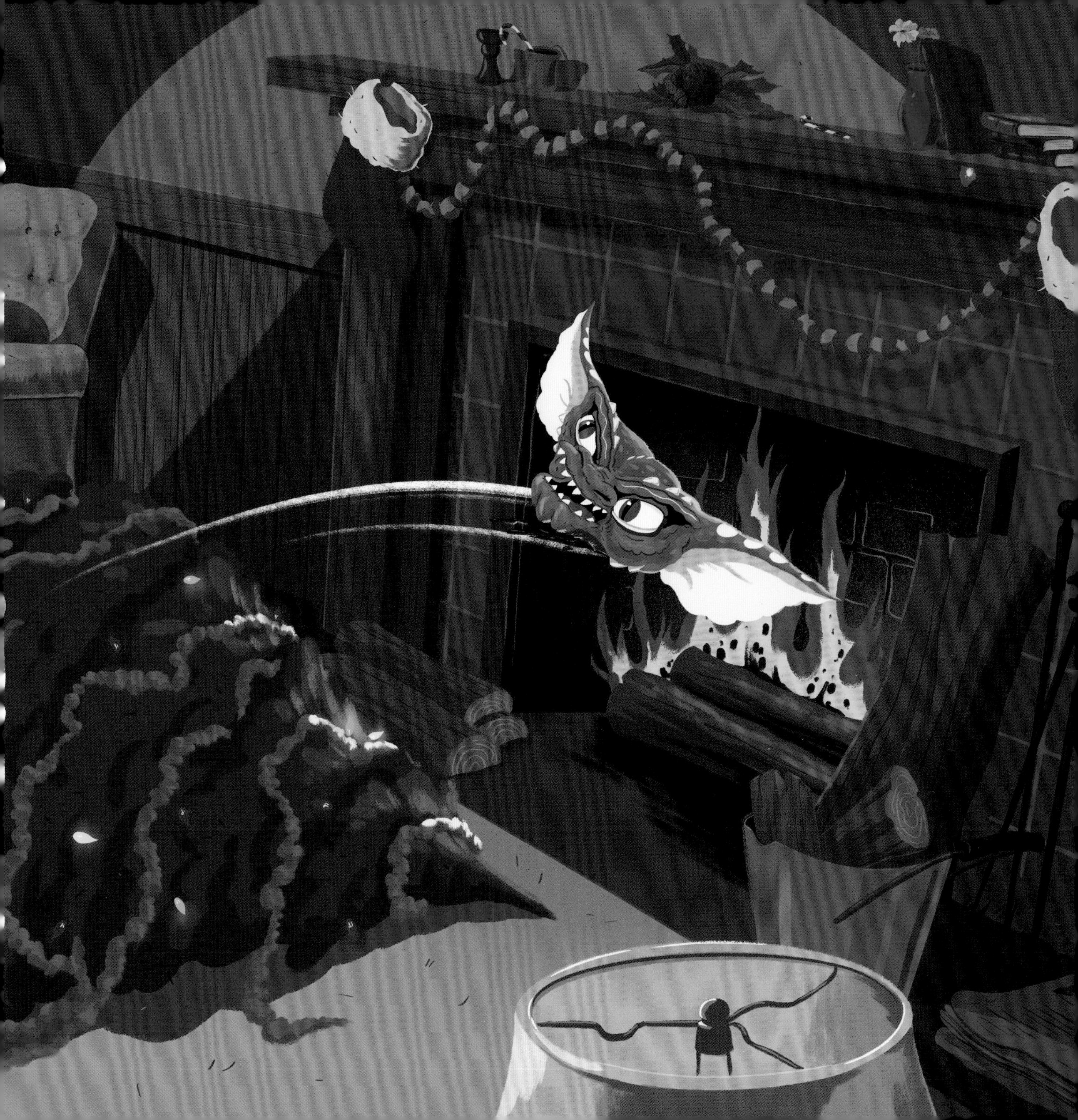

ON THE EIGHTH DAY OF CHRISTMAS, THE ONE CALLED STRIPE DID FLEE—
Footprints a-leading
To our next meeting.
At least he's not eating—
CRAP, THERE'S A POOL!

Stripe leaping out.
Yikes! That hurts.
One cannonball
And a pool bubbling ominously.

ON THE NINTH DAY OF CHRISTMAS, THEY'RE ON A KILLING SPREE.

Gremlins a-plowing,
Police a-doubting,
Kingston Falls is screaming,
Deagle's a-bleeding—
WAIT—NO, SHE'S DEAD!

IT'S SUPPOSED TO BE CHRISTMAS, FRANK!

Two stoplights screwed,
One flipped car,
Freak mailbox death,
And a Gremlin laughing maniacally.

ON THE TENTH DAY OF CHRISTMAS, AT DORRY'S I DID SEE:
Monsters a-flying.
Good, Kate's not dying.
Smoking and fighting,
Drinking and biting,
Cigarette lighting—
AND NONE SHOWED I.D.!

ASTRO
PEW PEW

Quick! Out the front.
Kate, you look nice—
Right, not the time—
Run for it, on the count of three!

ON THE ELEVENTH DAY OF CHRISTMAS,
In the movie mezzanine,

Snow White is showing,
Gremlins heigh-ho-ing,
Much popcorn throwing,
Aisles overflowing,
Chaos is growing,
No sign of slowing—

LET'S BLOW THEM UP!

To the boiler room!
Must go quick,
Release the gas,
And make a break for the alley.

ON THE TWELFTH DAY OF CHRISTMAS . . . YOU'RE FREAKING KIDDING ME! . . .

That's Stripe, the leader.
Why's he not dead yet?
Guess we should fix that . . .

But he's got a crossbow
And, oh God, a chain saw
Heading for the fountain.
Someone please stop him—
GIZMO SAVES THE DAY!

Two popping eyes,
Lots of slime,
Skin melting off—
Did they really go and make this PG?

ON THE LAST DAY OF CHRISTMAS—OH HEY, IT'S MR. WING.
This story's over
At least until the second movie!

INSIGHT EDITIONS

PO Box 3088
San Rafael, CA 94912
www.insighteditions.com

Find us on Facebook: www.facebook.com/InsightEditions
Follow us on Twitter: @insighteditions

Library of Congress Cataloging-in-Publication Data available.

ISBN: 978-1-64722-120-1

Publisher: Raoul Goff
Associate Publisher: Vanessa Lopez
Creative Director: Chrissy Kwasnik
VP of Manufacturing: Alix Nicholaeff
Designer: Lola Villanueva
Senior Editor: Amanda Ng
Editorial Assistant: Maya Alpert
Managing Editor: Lauren LePera
Production Editor: Jennifer Bentham
Senior Production Manager: Greg Steffen

Illustrations by JJ Harrison

Insight Editions, in association with Roots of Peace, will plant two trees for each tree used in the manufacturing of this book. Roots of Peace is an internationally renowned humanitarian organization dedicated to eradicating land mines worldwide and converting war-torn lands into productive farms and wildlife habitats. Roots of Peace will plant two million fruit and nut trees in Afghanistan and provide farmers there with the skills and support necessary for sustainable land use.

Manufactured in China by Insight Editions

10 9 8 7 6 5 4 3 2 1